Spring for Sophie

Yael Werber

Illustrated by Jen Hill

SCHOLASTIC INC.

ISBN 978-1-338-28507-9

12 11 10 9 8 7 6 5 4 3 2 1   18 19 20 21 22 23

Printed in the U.S.A.   40

First Scholastic printing, February 2018

Book design by Chloë Foglia
The text for this book was set in Dutch Mediaeval.
The illustrations for this book were rendered in gouache with digital retouching.

To my inner circle, who cheered me on the
whole way, but especially for my parents, who
have been cheering me on since day one.
—Y. W.

For Susie, a gifted puddle splasher.
—J. H.

"When will spring be here?" Sophie asked her mom.
"Spring comes slowly," her mom told her.
"How will I know when spring is coming?"

"The first way to tell if spring is coming is to listen for it. When you hear the birds start to sing their songs to each other, that's when you'll know spring is coming. That's what spring sounds like."

So, Sophie listened.

She listened in the mornings when she played with her sister in the snow,

and she listened in the evenings when she helped her dad collect wood for the fire.

At first she couldn't hear anything, except for
how quiet the world was when it was covered in
snow. But one day as she walked with her mom
to get the mail, she heard the first chirps!

Every day she heard more and more. First the chickadees, and then the mourning doves and the robins.

Soon she could hear all kinds
of birds calling to each other,
announcing that spring was
coming!

But outside it was still snowy and cold.

"How will I know when spring is getting even closer?" Sophie asked.

"You'll have to use your feet," her dad said. "When you start to feel the ground get softer and muddy, that's when you'll know spring is getting even closer. That's what spring feels like."

So, Sophie paid
extra attention
to her feet.

When she walked in the woods with her dad, the ground was still slippery and hard, and she had to hold her dad's hand.

When she walked Shadow with her mom, everything still felt icy. But then one day, the ground felt softer than before, and the snow was slushier, and pretty soon her boots started sinking into the ground instead of slipping on top of it.

Sophie felt
spring
getting closer.

"But it's still not spring," Sophie said, and she sighed when she had to put on her hat and gloves to go outside. "How will I know when spring is really here?"

"Well, Sophie, you'll have to use your eyes and nose to tell if spring is here," her mom said. "You'll have to watch and wait until you see the snow start to melt. And you will have to wait until the air begins to smell like earth and rain. That's when you'll know spring is here. That's what spring looks and smells like."

So, Sophie watched.

She watched as the ice melted off the lake,

and as the snow turned to puddles in her yard.

She watched as flowers pushed
up from under the ground and
showed their stems,

and she watched as new moss
covered the rocks in the woods.

She saw the world turn from white . . .

. . . to green.

And then one day, after the snow had melted, Sophie smelled the air.
She quickly put on her rain boots and raincoat, and ran outside.

Sophie looked up at the sky as the rain started to fall.
"Sophie! What are you doing?" she heard her dad call.

Sophie stuck out her tongue to catch the raindrops.

"Now I know spring is here!" she called.
"Because this is what spring tastes like!"